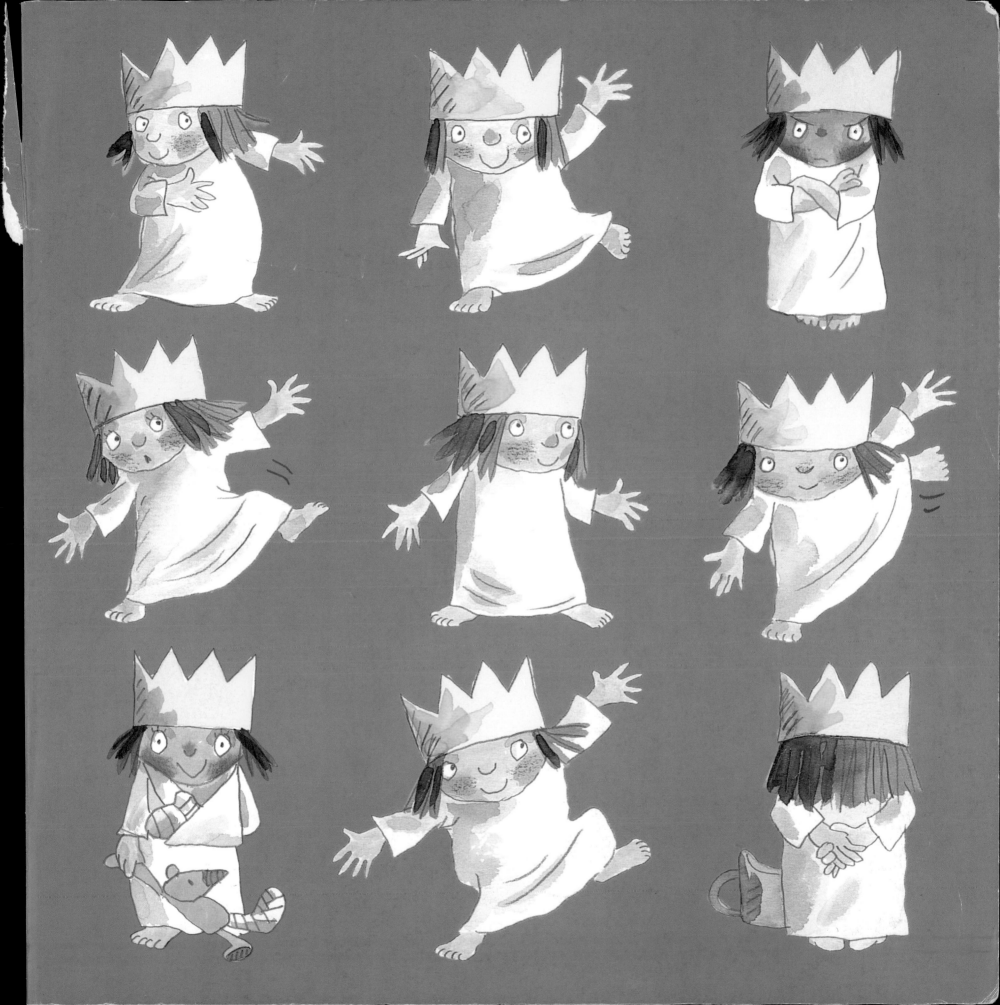

First published in hardback in Great Britain by Andersen Press Ltd in 1986
First published in paperback by Picture Lions in 1987
New edition published by Collins Picture Books in 2001
This edition published by HarperCollins Children's Books in 2006

5 7 9 10 8 6

ISBN-13: 978-0-00-723621-3

Picture Lions and Collins Picture Books are imprints of the Children's Division, part of HarperCollins Publishers Ltd.
HarperCollins Children's Books is a division of HarperCollins Publishers Ltd.

Text and illustrations copyright © Tony Ross 1986, 2001

Visit our website at: www.harpercollins.co.uk
Printed and bound by Leo Paper Products Ltd

I Want My Potty

Tony Ross

HarperCollins *Children's Books*

"Nappies are YUUECH!" said the Little Princess.
"There MUST be something better!"

"The potty's the place," said the Queen.

At first the Little Princess thought
the potty was worse.

"THE POTTY'S THE PLACE!" said the Queen.

So... the Little Princess had to learn.

Sometimes the Little Princess was a long way from
the potty when she needed it most.

Sometimes the Little Princess played tricks on the potty...

...and sometimes the potty played tricks on the Little Princess.

Soon the potty was fun

and the Little Princess loved it.

Everybody said the Little Princess was clever and
would grow up to be a wonderful queen.

"The potty's the place!"
said the Little Princess proudly.

One day the Little Princess was playing at the
top of the castle... when...

"I WANT MY POTTY!" she cried.

"She wants her potty," cried the Maid.

"She wants her potty," cried the King.

"She wants her potty," cried the Cook.

"She wants her potty," cried the Gardener.

"She wants her potty," cried the General.

"I know where it is," cried the Admiral.

So the potty was taken as quickly as possible

to the Little Princess... just...

...a little too late.